John Jamieson

The Sorrows of Slavery

A Poem

John Jamieson

The Sorrows of Slavery
A Poem

ISBN/EAN: 9783337121921

Printed in Europe, USA, Canada, Australia, Japan

Cover: Foto ©Andreas Hilbeck / pixelio.de

More available books at **www.hansebooks.com**

THE

SORROWS OF SLAVERY,

A POEM.

CONTAINING A

FAITHFUL STATEMENT OF FACTS

RESPECTING THE

AFRICAN SLAVE TRADE.

────────────

By the Rev. J. JAMIESON,

A. M. F. A. S. S.

────────────

LONDON:
────
PRINTED FOR J. MURRAY, NO. 32, FLEET-STREET.

────

1789.

ADVERTISEMENT.

THE principal design of the Author hath been to represent simple historical facts in the language of poetry; as this might attract the attention of some who would not otherwise give themselves the trouble of looking into the subject. Through the whole of the poem he hath carefully avoided exaggeration. Circumstances are faithfully stated from different publications, particularly those of the Rev. Messrs. Ramsay, Clarkson, Newton, and Nicholls; and of Mr. Falconbridge, Surgeon. The poem is divided into

*three parts, according to the natural divi-
sion of the subject : the first containing a
description of the methods used to procure
slaves on the Guinea Coast ; the second, of
their treatment on the Middle Passage ; and
the third, of their situation in the West-
Indies.*

ARGUMENT.

PART I.

ADDRESS to the Ladies of Britain, claiming their attention to this mournful theme, as in all refpects worthy of the exercife of their tender feelings.—Invocation.—Sailing of the Guinea fhips.—Meafures adopted by the African princes for fupplying their demands.—Various arts practifed by the Black traders.—Defcription of a flave-market.—Juft retribution of Providence in the fate of many of the Black traders themfelves.—Progrefs of the flaves from the fairs to the fhips.

PART II.

Situation of the flaves on board.----Attempts to deftroy themfelves.--- Affecting ftory of Calabar, from Mr. Clarkfon's Treatife on the Slavery and Commerce of the Human Species *.----Reflections

* Since the Poem went to prefs, the Author has feen an authentic copy of the depofitions of *William Floyd* of Briftol, mariner, and of *Little Ephraim Robin John*, and *Ancona Robin Robin John*, of Calabar, with refpect to this affair, taken at Briftol, 30th

addreffed to the Guinea merchants.----Sufferings of the flaves on board.----Story of Zilia.----Infurrection.----Treatment of the unfuccefsful infurgents.----Conjectures of the Negroes as to their fate.

PART III.

Arrival in the iflands.----Preparation of the flaves.----Different modes of fale. Vendue. Scramble.----Fate of thofe who are unfit for the market.----Interview between a Servant of Jefus and fome Negroes.----Story of Calypfo.----Ideas of Chriftianity entertained by the flaves.----Treatment in the plantations.----Addrefs to the American States,----to Britons,----to our honourable Reprefentatives in Parliament.----The iniquity of this traffic demonftrated from various denunciations in the Divine Law.

September and 9th November, 1773. With thefe the account given in the Poem agrees in all the leading circumftances. But there are feveral others mentioned which confiderably aggravate the villainy of the perpetrators.

SORROWS

OF

SLAVERY.

PART I.

Ye British fair, whofe gentle bofoms heave
The figh of pity at the tale of woe ;
Whofe lovely eyes, like fun-beams darting thro'
A watery cloud, the rofes underneath
In fweet profufion fcatter'd oft bedew,
And lend new grace to ev'ry varying tinge ;
Why purchafe forrow in the tragic fcene,
Or court it in the fancy-labour'd tale,
Why like a mother, in her frenzy fad
Who hugs the pillow for her clay-cold babe,
The formlefs child of fiction fendly nurfe,

B

And wifh it real, that its mifery
May every hidden wheel of mercy move :
A real tragedy, unmatch'd in fong,
While Afric forces on your fight averfe ;
Where every village opes a difmal fcene,
Where acts of death unnumber'd chill the foul,
And freeborn Britons act the bloodieft parts ?
The treafures of benevolence in vain
Why thus exhauft ? Why Pity's thrilling cords,
That twift around your hearts, fo idly rack,
While up her fable curtain Afric draws,
Difclofing many a Werter loft to fame,
Whofe harrowing tale is only wrote in blood ;
And many a Defdemona, who not needs
A Shakefpeare to defcribe her woes unjuft,
Nor craves a Siddons to call forth your tears ?

   They are not fair like you. But can the hues
Of Nature various tinge the fecret foul ?
Say, does not the alembic of their hearts
As pure Compaffion's genial drops diftil
As your's ? Oft do they not o'erflow
The cifterns of their eye-lids too confin'd ?
Does Grief ne'er wring their heart-ftrings ? Or can
    Pain

Make no nerve thrill? In that warm clime alone
Does Love's electric fire shoot thro' no vein,
Rapid, resistless, hurrying on the blood,
As its elastic channels it would burst?
Of cruel absence finds no lover there
The saddening influence? Can he, in his heart,
That void insufferable never feel,
Thou oft, fair maid, hast felt; a void so great,
A world, without the object lov'd, to fill
Is far too little? He hath felt it too.
To him his dusky mistrefs is as fair
As thou art to thy lover; fairer far
Than thou, with all thy changeling-charms, wouldst
    prove.
Is there no mother here, whose melting heart
Darts thro' her eye, when smiling on her babe;
Who fondly strains her empty breast to yield
Those drops reluctant famine yet hath spar'd;
Or feels new pangs more piercing than the first,
From its fond claspings sever'd by the sword?
Superior rank if thy complexion plead
In Nature's scale, the justice of its plea
Let the superior brightness of thy soul,
Let Nature's first-born, gentle Pity, show.

No fabled Mufe I fummon to my aid :
The fong of truth fuch aid ignoble fcorns.
O Thou, Almighty Father ! who haft made
Of one blood all the nations, and affign'd
To each on this thy earth his feveral fpot,
Who from thy height tranfcendant deign'ft to look
On all the various fons of men, and own
All as thy offspring, blacken'd by thy fun,
Or by thy fnows made white, to Thee alike :
Infpire me, while I fing the general rights
Of human kind, and mourn the inroads fell
Man, thy poor vaffal, dares to make on man.
From Thee this fong begins, All-powerful Foe
Of Tyrants, who Thy image great debafe,
And thro' Thy image aim a thruft at Thee.
This fong is thine ; for Thou at firft on man
The precious gift of Liberty beftowd'ft,
And in thy love unparallel'd at length
Didft fend thy Image, perfect as Thyfelf,
To purchafe Liberty for man enflav'd,
Ev'n in man's nature, and proclaim this boon,
Worthy of Heaven, to ev'ry race of man.
Infpire my lay, and of humanity
Let th' infpiration blefs'd thro' Britain's Ifle

Spread like the fire the wither'd heath that burns!
For what are all oblations made to Thee
Without humanity? Intrufion grofs,
A daring infult to the God of Love,
Who claims this proof of love to him fincere;
That, like the vapours rais'd from earth to heav'n,
To blefs the earth more genial it return.

From Avon's ftream the bounding veffels pour,
By profperous gales invited to the main.
Their fails expanded, every breeze embrace,
And wing their way to Afric's arid fhore.
Meanwhile the various defpots of her foil,
Impatient for the vifit yearly paid
By ftrangers, to the eye alone more fair
Than they, and envious of the fhort-liv'd peace
Their vaffals owe to Europe's gentler ftorms,
Ope every fluice of war, and thofe burnt fands,
That thirft in vain for water, drench in blood.

Not Gallia, tho' for politics far-fam'd,
Half the inventive faculty can boaft
In framing reafons for illicit war,
Or can fo fage apologies devife
For breach of faith, where greedy intereft claims
The death of thoufands for a Tyrant's meal.

'Tis not a thirſt for fame impels to war
The numerous Chiefs that rule theſe parched plains.
Tho' baſe this appetite, in balance weigh'd
Againſt the blifs of millions, baſer ſtill
What wakes the maddening rage of battle here.
The idol-caſk is empty, that contain'd
The pleaſing poiſon brought from Britain's Iſle,
Which taught the Prince of Damu to forget
His cares, in ſweet intoxication drown'd.
What ſhall the lofs ſupply?   A thouſand lives
Are naught in value to a Monarch's dream.
Tho' every drop ſhould as its price demand
The copious tide of life that idly flows
Around a vaſſal-heart, 'tis not too dear,
When greatly paid a Monarch's thirſt to quench.
Forthwith his ſable legions he convenes,
And arms for war. 'Gainſt Aſou, neighbouring prince
And friend of youth, by ſolemn oaths ally'd,
In peace rejoicing, unſuſpicious, proud
Of friendſhip never by a frown impair'd,
He ruſhes on relentlefs.   In his train
A thouſand angels of deſtruction aim
Their ſhafts unerring.   Nor complains the Chief
Tho' every life, unmercifully ſpar'd

To linger out in Slavery's death prolong'd,
And only by the force of fetters held
In cruel durance, cofts a tenfold death.

By Europe's luxury themfelves enflav'd,
Opprefs'd with wants their fathers never knew,
Thefe little fovereigns quarrels often feign
In concert, that by fines reciprocal,
In bloodlefs victims only to be paid,
Their mighty mutual wrath may be appeas'd.

Believe not, injur'd Briton, the falfe tales.
Of credulous fools or flaves of Avarice.
Its dread tribunal Africa can boaft,
Where criminals to flavery are condemn'd.
But tho' erected in the awful name
Of heaven-born Juftice, often is it not
To tread her under foot, or while fhe's woo'd
With folemn mockery, to make of her
A very harlot, and her fhame increafe
By feeming honour; Juftice to transform,
By hell-born arts, into Iniquity?
Here thofe are often doom'd for fouleft crimes,
Whofe fpotlefs innocence the Judge well knows.
New crimes are artfully devis'd; new laws
Are daily fram'd for thofe more venial far

Than any yet in papal lifts enroll'd;
The code fill growing with the Monarch's wants:
And oft the crime is older than the law.

But is the call too urgent for delay?
All palliatives are fcorn'd; the Prince's need
Ev'ry expedient fully fanctifies.
Thro' every facred, focial tie at once
He boldly burfts. See! where Dahomy's king,
In midft of night and darknefs ominous,
His gloomy fpoilers crouding after him
In dreadful filence, like fome demon fell
From outer darknefs loos'd for man's deftruction,
Flies to a village of his own domain,
His fatal torch blue-gleaming in his hand,
Of death dire meteor! Sacrilegious wretch!
Dar'ft thou apply it?   Ah! the deed is done.
The wavering flames, now towering high, on heav'n
A horrid luftre throw; anon they fink,
As confcious of its more than midnight-frown.
The peaceful habitants, in horrors wak'd,
In vain attempt to fly.   Here flames purfue;
And there a foe unknown, with pointed fteel,
Their flight withftands.   Some eager to efcape,
In ftupefaction rufh'd amidft the flames:

While fome, of half its terrors death to rob,
That fate leaft lingering greedily embrace.
What fhrieks of mifery rend the wondering fky,
Mix'd with the bellowing of the raging fire,
And howlings of the fpoilers mercilefs!
Here mothers, frantic, fearlefs of the flames,
Burft thro' their volumes, fearching for their babes,
For ever to their fond endearments loft;
To their primeval principles reduc'd,
Amidft the burning, undiftinguifh'd mafs:
And now they Heav'n implore, and then accufe.
There, children trembling with an orphan heart,
Their parents dear, infirm, decrept with age,
Strive to difcover; by their piercing cries
In pity melted, or to madnefs rous'd.
Heard fo diftinctly are their fhrieks of woe
Amid the ruins wide, as to provoke
To mournful fellowfhip in death the fons,
But not to fave the fires. What tenfold grief
The remnant refcued from the flames awaits?
Already reft of all that man holds dear;
Bound by their countrymen, their kinfmen, friends,
In hated chains, at their own King's command;
Their fouls indignant burn to meet the flames

c

They bafely fled, not half fo keen as thofe
That now confume them inly, and to mix
With kindred fpirits in their flight ferene
To realms of liberty.   It wounds them more
Life from their native Sovereign to receive
At fuch expence, than death in fiery form
Had pow'r to wound, the ravager unknown.

If fuch the ways of him whom Nature calls
The Father of his People, rais'd by Heav'n
To guard them from Oppreffion's iron rod ;
Why, Britons, wonder that fome vaffals bafe
Their humble treading in his path fhould deem
No heinous mifdemeanour, or that they
Should one more proper for themfelves devife ?

Oft, child of Freedom, in thy favour'd ifle,
The numerous herds of cattle thou haft feen
To market driven, with heat and thirft annoy'd,
Lowing and panting, while the cruel lafh
Urg'd their reluctant pace.   Thy fellow-men
Thus brutify'd thy darkening eyes ne'er faw.
But fuch the profpect Negroland prefents.
To human markets, regularly held,
The traffickers in human flefh repair ;
In flefh alone, for here the nobler foul

Nor raifes, nor diminifhes the price.

Tho' train'd by ftrangers to the horrid art,

Thofe are not ftrangers now by thee obferv'd.

The fons of Afric trade in Afric's fons.

With what infulting coolnefs they proceed !

See ! how they creep along the lengthen'd ranks,

Each naked captive, with a fcrupulous eye

Surveying, as they would a fenfelefs brute.

Mark ! how their brethren they in worth debafe !

" This one is lean, and that one feebly walks;

" This fmooth-fkin'd fellow toil has never known;

" That pregnant woman by the road will die."——

They dodge, and lie, and fwear the market low :

By every jockeying trick degrading man.

Left any fault lie hid, each trembling limb

They roughly prefs, and turn them round and
        round,

Without regard to fex.   O ! Modefty ;

'Twere profanation fcarce to be aton'd

In fuch a tale to fpeak thy virgin name !

    Inhuman monfters !——Ha ! I've gone too far.

I Britifh ears may daringly offend.

Thefe dufky merchants are but caterers

For other men, the pimps of Europe's luft ;

And Heathens too, in blindnefs who fulfil
The orders by enlighten'd Chriftians giv'n.
Yes, Britain, thefe are thy blefs'd profelytes,
Proficients wond'rous in that glorious path
Without thy *zeal* to Afric fcarcely known.

   " But whence," doft thou enquire, " this wafte of
       men ?
" What fertile land, of nations ample hive,
" Can conftantly from its exuberance vaft
" Pour forth ten times ten thoufand every year ?
" Are they in certain diftricts bred for fale
" As we breed cattle, fons of flavifh race ?"²

   O Britain ! oft by neighb'ring nations dup'd,
But here by thy unnatural fons alone ;
How long believe thofe filly tales that owe
To Avarice, juggling and carnivorous,
Their form mif-fhapen, and the offspring fair
Of candid Truth and weeping Mercy fcorn ?

   From various climes thefe wretched captives come,
Where never European wanderer trode,
From climes to geographic fkill unknown.
Oft, ere the general rendezvous they reach,
The changeful property of divers lords,
To real or pretended crimes, while fome

Owe lofs of freedom, far the greateft part,
To modes of capture fcorn'd by nobler brutes.
In thefe extenfive regions hundreds live
By ravifhing th' unwary, or the weak;
Men-ftealers by profeffion, who the purfe,
Not as its owner half fo much regard.
Mark in yon file the young and handfome maid,
Whofe eyes have form'd a rivulet on her breaft.
Returning from a fcene of feftive joy,
While thro' the lingering twilight eve's bright ftar
On earth had hardly glanc'd, within a cry
Of her companions, near her father's houfe,
A villain from a thicket rufh'd upon her,
And dragg'd her off; threat'ning with dreadful oaths
Death inftantaneous, if fhe gave one cry.
See, nigh her, one who hugs her fcreaming babe
With fond anxiety. Well may'ft thou hug,
Difconfolate mother! for it coft thee dear.
To bathe it in the cooling ftream fhe went;
But while fhe fportive prefs'd the lambent wave,
A tyger hideous, in man's form difguis'd,
Sprung on her from amid the ruftling reeds,
Where he from morn to eve had lurk'd for prey.
Ah! wretched, for ftill greater woes referv'd!

Ev'n now a ruffian trader pays thy price
Reluctant, but thy precious load excludes.
In vain thofe fhrieks, in vain doft beat thy breaft,
Doom'd never more to fuckle thy lov'd babe.
Wrung from thy folding arms by ruthlefs hands,
Thy fole folace for ever muft thou leave!

   Behold that king-like man, whofe fleecy head
Grey Time has bleach'd, whofe rough cheek he hath
      plough'd.
Befide him ftands his fon, a finewy youth,
Who from his cloud of darknefs darts a fmile
Contemptuous on his fneaking purchafer.
Invited to a neighbouring hamlet's feaft,
They unfufpicious went, and pafs'd the day
In focial mirth and rural luxury.
But as they backward trac'd their well known way,
Their faithlefs hoft and bafe confederates
Their darkening path with treach'rous purpofe
      mark'd.
Soon did they overpow'r the feeble fire;
Not fo the fon.   Thou feeft his cheek deep-fcar'd.
He mow'd his enemies, as a fportive boy,
Pleas'd with his prowefs, would the thiftle's beard.
Soon had he routed them, and loos'd the thongs

That bound his father; but their ftanch-mouth'd
   dogs,
Taught for the purpofe, from their litter train'd
To blood, and kept for baiting men alone,
He could not hold at bay. Hence thefe deep fcars,
And fuch the battles moft of thefe have fought.
   Ye ruthlefs ravifhers! whofe prey is man,
Admire the juftice of All-feeing Heav'n,
That marks you as the victims of its ire,
You oft entangling in the fatal fnare
For others laid, and for your courfe prolong'd
In villainy, as pledge of payment full,
Wrenching the yoke round your own ftubborn necks.
Why pity crave? What heart would lavifh it
On you, whofe bowels ne'er in pity yearn'd?
Your parents, brothers, wives, and warlike fons,
While by the fecret influence of Heaven
Their powers are all to non-refiftance lull'd,
With filent awe your righteous fate confefs,
Oft by their confcious boding hearts foretold!
And ye, who by your fov'reign, lion-like,
As his jackals infidious, have been hir'd
To fill the royal glutton's ravenous maw,
Repine not, though, when in your ravage wide

By force fuperior ftay'd, he you difown,
To his own pow'rs of credence give the lie,
And fell you with the flaves yourfelves have fnar'd.
Fools! is not this the Tyrant's laft reward;
His parting pledge of gratitude, the coin
In which he liquidates fuch fwelling debts?
Are you the firft of traitors thus betray'd?
The only motive ftill hath intereft been;
To your's alike: and could you ever dream
That he his own would facrifice for your's?
He breaks his faith; but who can faith expect
In intercourfe that for its bafis owns
The abjuration of its very name?

   Now from the field of purchafe flowly moves
The troop reluctant, tottering every ftep
Beneath the cumb'rous, forked yoke that binds
Each in fucceffion to the flave before,
Throughout the mournful, far extending file.
Each back is with the fuftenance deprefs'd
Ungrateful life unwillingly requires,
Dragg'd on thro' tedious defarts, which nor bread
Nor water yield, nor human footfteps fhew.
From various regions pillag'd, and from tongues
That no alliance claim, they in their march

The mournful confolation often want
Of fond Narration's interchange of woes.
Each bears in partnerfhip his neighbour's yoke,
But cannot lighten his moft preffing load
By fadly-pleafing fellowfhip in grief.
In bags, fufpended from their deep-gall'd necks,
Of helplefs babes the fuperadded load
Enfeebled mothers bear.   Some big with child,
The cries of famine, grief, fatigue, defpair,
With thofe of parturition, void of hope,
In melancholy fymphony conjoin:
No hufband near to minifter folace,
Or make the agonizing mother deem
Thofe fufferings blefs'd, a living pledge that yield
Of faithful, mutual love : no father fond
To hug and blefs his puling, paffive babe !
The only cordial to her fainting heart
Of putrid water a few drops fupply.
Ev'n now a travailling woman's cries I hear;
And fuch the mournful ftrains in which her child
Firft-born fhe welcomes into hated day :
" With tranfport many a woman would a fon
" Behold, and all her pangs anon forget ;
" But I unhappy muft the barren blefs,

" And view my womb's fruit as my greateſt curſe,

" In ripeneſs dropt into this world's wide field,

" But to be cruſh'd by ſtern Oppreſſion's tread.

" Thrice happy they, whoſe fruit hath in the bud

" By ſome propitious blaſt been kindly nipt !

" But thou, my 'harmleſs, once long-wiſh'd-for
        babe,

" Art to thy wretched mother a new ſource

" Of endleſs ſorrows, far more ſharp than thoſe

" Late uſhering thee into this ſcene of woe !"

Some onward trudge, in ſullen ſorrow whelm'd,

Revolving gloomy purpoſes within

The dark receſſes of their troubled ſouls ;

Not deign they with one ſolitary groan

To grace the triumph of their ſavage foes :

While they, whoſe anguiſh more tempeſtuous, like

Deep-cavern'd waves, by ſecret winds enrag'd,

Burſts foaming from their mouths with mercileſs
        laſh,

To all their juſt reproaches no reply

Receive, but what the cruel gag affords,

The mute confeſſor of a cauſe accurs'd.

With hunger, thirſt, and anguiſh overpower'd,

One ſwoons, and, ſenſeleſs, to the ground would
        ſink,

Did not his yoke, by fellow-fufferers borne,
His drooping head fuftain, and drag along
His body motionlefs, by naught reftor'd
To feeling, but the poignancy of pain.
Another feems to fwoon, but not to him
Avails the barbarous remedy.   Grim Death,
Lefs cruel than his churlifh minifters,
Here in a moment of compaffion bland,
Burfts the clay cell, and bids the prifoner fly.
Sufpended is the march; but only 'till
The breathlefs corfe is from thofe fetters loos'd,
Already by its airy tenant fcorn'd.
The lump exanimate is from the yoke
Inhumanly dropt on its kindred foil,
And left without a fimple fhroud of duft
To hide it from the beafts and birds of prey.

When drowfy night her opiate kind prepares
To lull a world befides, one balmy drop
She fcarcely to thefe miferable deigns.
No more their limbs at liberty they tofs.
Not ev'n their dreams can Freedom's phantom fair
In mercy vifit, with illufion bleft.
Ingenious Avarice hath charms devis'd
To exorcife this fpirit, to its peace

So unpropitious.   To 'ie maffive yoke,
Their arms outſtretch'd in forc'd embraces cling;
As ſleeping ſlaves the oars they're chain'd to hug.

    For many moons the weak ſurvivors plod
The howling waſte, in numbers waning ſtill :
Not of the period of their pilgrimage
Preſuming one conjecture vague to form ;
Nor conſcious of the greatly-fear'd event,
That may its awful conſummation prove.
At length, another waſte of waters meets
Their eye aſtoniſh'd, endleſs to the view,
Unequal, like their native rivers now
Serenely ſmiling; ſuddenly enrag'd,
In mountains riſing, as it dar'd to laſh
The frowning ſky.   What terrors new appal,
When brooding o'er the trembling deep they ſpy
A monſter wing'd, in its tremendous form
Unmatch'd by all their wilds or waters yield,
From its ſtrong ligaments ſtruggling to break looſe,
And gaping to devour them as its prey !
They ſhuddering turn, and gaze, as if a ray
Of Hope might dart from ſome bleſt ſpace unknown,
Hope's boundaries far beyond ; but gaze in vain.
They heav'n aſſail with looks of menace proud,

Provoking its lefs dreaded thunderbolts
To end their miferies.   Then on earth they frown
With piercing eyes of fury, as they dar'd
Its dreadful mouth to open and devour.
Anon are open'd all the fprings of grief,
Half-dry'd by conftant running : all their gods
They raving fupplicate ; they wring their hands,
And beat their breafts, and tear their trembling limbs.
But vain thefe tranfports ; dragg'd or goaded on,
'Till by the ravening monfter gorg'd at once,
They fhrink with horror ftill to feel alive.

 Some down the rivers in the light canoe
Are hurried to the coaft.   Bound hand and foot,
They to the leaky bottom are confign'd,
Where day and night in filthy water drench'd,
They bafely lie, like nature's offals vile.
What can the filly pomp of flags difplay'd,
Or mufic's joy prepofterous avail,
But Mifery's fenfibility to wake,
And wound afrefh by Scorn's empoifon'd fting?

 A new furvey thefe wretches muft endure
Before the haughty franger, whofe ftern word
Hath made them captives, and who feems to count
The condefcenfion infinite, that bids

Such caitiffs under *him* ftill wear their chains.

Thofe whom Difeafe relentlefs, Famine's rage,

Or ceafelefs toil hath pin'd ; whom Nature's hand

Hath roughly touch'd in their formation hid,

Or cruel accident hath marr'd ; whom age

Hath fhrivell'd ; or whom chains have lam'd,

Are fcornfully rejected.   Curfes fell

Are by their owner on their guiltlefs heads

Invok'd, as if their mifery were their crime.

In mercilefs ftripes oft breaks his fury forth.

Not feldom, every other price refus'd,

The horrid price of their offencelefs blood,

Shed inftantly, alone can reimburfe

The Tyrant's cofts, and glut his fell revenge.

But ftill th' unnatural cargo to complete,

New plans of villainy muft be effay'd.

Some paddling round the veffel, her ftrange bulk

Admiring, fearlefs of deceit, are feiz'd.

Some, while they wifh to barter Afric's wealth

For Europe's toys.   By invitation kind •

From the perfidious fons of Ocean, fome

Allur'd, the floating prifon gaily tempt,

Ne'er to revifit their beloved fhore.

The treacherous beverage of the ftranger lulls

To pleafing ftupor; foon they wake in chains,
Robb'd of that precious bleffing Lethe's draught
Might in oblivion drown, but not reftore.

PART II.

ΛT length they from their moorings flowly
    loofe,
Their fails unfurl to the propitious breeze,
And fhape their courfe to Caribbean Ifles.
Like undiftinguifh'd lumber in their hold,
Between the decks the living cargo's ftow'd;
Forming, like fome ant-hill, a moving heap;
Tho' not, like its laborious tenants, free.
The galling fetters each to each confine,
Their legs and arms enclofing in rude grafp.
Oft alfo is the haughty neck enchain'd.
They every motion by confent muft make;
Frequent in quarrels, when their Babel-tongues
The biting of diftorted chains provoke.
For fo inventive is the cruelty
Of their harfh jailors; as if fimple bonds,
To guiltlefs negroes were a boon too great;
Tranfverfely they are bound, in ftudied forms
Moft adverfe to the fuffering captive's cafe.

No place to ftretch their torpid limbs they find,
And fcarce to lie ; convolv'd they rather feem.
At morn, to tafte the healthful breeze, on deck
They're roughly fummon'd. Ev'n ftern Cruelty
At times to fhuffling Avarice homage yields :
But ftill a frown its greateft favour clouds.
Of Freedom this merc fhadow, to the deck
The chains that rudely rivet them, efface.
There, rang'd in mournful ranks, they faintly fpy
Their much-lov'd country flying from their view,
As if afham'd to own them as her fons.
What fhrieks of grief unbridled, of defpair
Deep groans and hideous yells the welkin rend !
Heav'n's tempefts rude in madnefs they invoke
To blefs with fhipwreck, that their mangled limbs
At leaft may once more kifs the darling ftrand.

See ! where one, watchful of the moment kind,
When from the ring-bolts loos'd to leave the deck,
Leaps overboard, the partner of his chains,
Of life lefs lavifh, dragging after him ;
And fills a monftrous fhark's deep-forked jaws,
Expanding to receive its fhrinking prey.

All fuftenance fome obftinately fcorn.
If dreadful threats avail not to fubdue,

E

On their weak limbs, while pinion'd to the maft,

In mercilefs repetition, the keen fcourge

Draws its deep furrows.   If they ftill refufe,

Wrench'd open are their parched mouths, and down

Their throats reluctant are the liquid means

Of life pour'd violently.   Their lips at times

Th' embrace confuming of live coals endure.

But ineffectual oft thefe cruelties;

The wretches find that death they long have fought

With unabated ardor, and acquir'd

At fuch expence of fuffering exquifite;

Firmly refolv'd, by vengeance on themfelves,

At laft on their oppreffors to be veng'd.

    Among the mournful groupe a captive lay,

Whofe fullen greatnefs told his former ftate.

Few words he utter'd; ftill the hollow groan

And eye indignant injur'd pride betray'd.

Oft did his chain mate urge him to reveal,

By what viciffitude of Fortune he

This deftiny had found.   With looks alone

Of ftubborn grief as often he reply'd.

One day, at length, half-melted into tears,

He thus the fulnefs of his foul effus'd.

    " My name is Ephraim, of the princely race

Of Calabar defcended, born to rule.
In friendfhip with the Englifh long I liv'd,
Their trade protected, and to Juftice gave
All who their ample rights to injure dar'd.
On others their impoftures frequent I
Reluctant faw; but confcioufnefs of right,
An unfufpicious foul, and more than thefe,
An unperceiv'd felf-partiality
My mental eye fo film'd, I ne'er could deem
That *me* they would deceive. A fatal grudge,
Between the ancient town of Calabar
And that the new yclep'd, of late prevail'd;
This execrable trade in man the caufe.
We old poffeffors frequently receiv'd
Kind letters from the Captains of the fleet,
Then in our river moor'd. In flattering ftrains
Our quarrels they lamented; all in one
Engaging, if their friendfhip we would prove,
Their fhips by entering as our bulwarks fure,
From every injury they would us defend;
And vowing that they only wifh'd to try
All gentle means th'unnatural breach to heal.

" I with my brother, many other Chiefs,
Of leading citizens a numerous fuite,

In ten canoes embark'd with heart-felt joy,
Bleffing the Heaven-fent minifters of peace.
Throughout the fleet difpers'd, the nobles, each
Had with officious care his place affign'd,
According to his rank. The reft meanwhile
On board receiv'd, or cluftering in their barks,
Foreftall'd the bleffings of returning peace.

" We exil'd brothers, in th' adjoining hall,
With pleafing hope the languid hours beguil'd,
And vied in praifing our protectors kind.
But horrid interruption! all at once
The ftern Commander, with his crew in arms,
Rufh'd in on us. We thro' the windows try'd
To force our way : but wounded, overpower'd,
And with amazement at the treafon dire
Benumb'd, our limbs their wonted pow'r forgot,
And feebly yielded to thefe fetters vile.
The veffel inftantly its dreadful flames
To vomit forth on our canoe begins.
The fell attack unable to fuftain,
From under its poffeffors foon it finks,
And leaves them ftruggling 'midft the fmoking gulph,
To flavery or death an inftant prey.
The bloody fignal forthwith every fhip

Repeats. The wretched refugees anon,
Unwarn'd of danger, are by it empal'd
On every fide. Some, whelm'd with their canoes,
At once the bottom reach to rife no more.
Others the mimic thunderbolt deftroys.
Some, flying from its vengeance, court the fhore,
Lefs fearing foes avow'd than perjur'd friends.

   " But now the fell confpiracy its deeps
Unfolds. The new inhabitants, forewarn'd
By their infernal allies, in their boats ·
The flying wretches now purfuing, leave
Their bufhy coverts, in canoes embark,
And with the thirft of kindred blood infpir'd
By Chriftians, to their fuppliant countrymen
Enfnar'd beyond efcape, with favage joy
The mercilefs hand of death alone outftretch.

   " Oh! Calabar belov'd, ne'er by thefe eyes
Again to be beheld, that fatal day
Well may'ft thou weep, and in thy lifts enrol,
As mark'd for vengeance by the hand of Heav'n,
Three hundred of thy nobleft fons it tore
From thy maternal arms, by flames deftroy'd,
By waters fwallow'd, or by chains debas'd.

   " Nor did this horrid facrifice fuffice,

The river yet was dy'd with blood, and ftrew'd
With mangled corfes ; when the hoftile Chiefs,
Whofe rage for blood, like that of ravening beafts,
The blood already fhed had only wak'd,
Before this fhip in their canoe appear'd,
My brother Amboe claiming as the price
Of their confederacy.   With generous warmth
He pray'd our rugged Tyrant not to burft
Thro' every tie of friendfhip, and of faith,
Nor yield to the relentlefs rage of foes
One who ne'er injur'd him, but often ferv'd,
The faithlefs Chriftian no intreaties move :
The noble Amboe, for a flave exchang'd,
Is from the proffer'd refuge headlong tofs'd.
Thefe eyes, in madnefs rolling, faw the deed
Infernal powers had blufh'd to perpetrate.
Why fhould I add what Nature fhrinks to tell,
To me tho' far lefs horrid than the paft?
Immediately, without the form of proof,
His head I from his body fever'd faw,
Unable to prevent or venge the blow.
Tho' with my brother, there in fetters bound,
The fate of guiltlefs Amboe I efcap'd,
As lefs obnoxious to our cruel foes ;

Yet wretched is the confolation left :
He dy'd a martyr'd noble, we live flaves."
    Thus fpoke the fallen Chief. A deep-fetch'd
    groan
The period of his mournful tale announc'd.
Ye Britifh Merchants, why with wonder ftare,
When now and then a veffel is cut off,
With alf its crew, on the Barbarian coaft ?
Why th' authors of this ruin execrate
As monfters in man's fafhion ? Are not ye
The parents fell of defolation wide
Through Afric's fhores and defarts unexplor'd ?
Is not your very trade a war proclaim'd
Againft man's nature ? Blufh then to refufe
To them reprifals, who have ne'er aggrefs'd.
Such vengeance is as natural to them,
As that againft their native beafts of prey
Directed, which their peaceful huts invade.
Their tygers and their lions fierce are ye.
The minifters of Heaven's fell vengeance they
As really are to you, as thofe of old
Who bore its dread commiffion to deftroy
Nations in guilt that ne'er with you might vie.
Their mental powers you fcorn : but fuch their fenfe

Of retribution, of that very crew
That injur'd them, the flow return they wait,
And mark it out for vengeance.   Does it fhun
The hoftile fhore?   In fubftitution they
A veffel from the felf fame port confign
To dread deftruction, fuddenly difcern'd,
Beyond miftake, by obfervation keen
Of thofe peculiarities that ftamp
On manners, or on tongues their forms minute.
    Ah! what a fcene of mifery lies hid
From Britifh eyes, below the hatches clofe,
While the poor flaves in fuffocation pant
Beneath the blaze of equatorial day!
When thro' th' uncover'd grate a breath of air
Its fcanty aid in pity feems to lend,
Tho' by the fteam exhaling half repell'd;
One trembling ftrives the falutary valve
To gain, but overcome by weaknefs, faints
Ere half his journey's o'er.   Another tempts
The fame adventure, dragging in his chains
His dead companion : but the noifome load
His ftrength furpaffing, to the ground he falls,
And in his fall a fellow-captive wounds.
The heat infufferable, putrid air,

Unwholefome viands, treatment mercilefs,
With never-ceafing anguifh, quickly prove
The certain harbingers of fell Difeafe,
Which, in its hafty ftrides, to many deigns
Emancipation from the hated yoke.
Thofe who furvive them, envious of their fate,
'Mid excremental filth and mucous blood
In dire pollution roll, like wounded beafts
Weltering amidft the noifome fhambles gore.

   Thine eye avert not, Briton delicate,
From this harfh picture. From the life 'tis drawn,
And drawn for thee, that in it thou may'ft trace
Thofe grifly features and diftorted limbs
That call thee parent, and thofe gaping wounds
Giv'n in the birth by thy unnatural hand;
Or if not giv'n, yet canker'd, widen'd, own'd
By thee, while to th' extreme of fkill and pow'r
Thy hand of mercy is not ftretch'd to heal.

   Behold that maid, poffefs'd of every charm
That Nature boafts, if regular lineaments
And faultlefs fymmetry contribute aught
To beauty's form; if in the various eye,
It beams or languifhes, commands or pleads
With rhetoric refiftlefs; in the mouth

If e'er it fmiles, or fpreads the toils of love
In playful dimples; if at once it awes
And captivates the heart in every look
And motion; if its fubtile effence lies
In framing to the comparative eye
Th' external image of a lovely foul,
Pure, noble, piteous and benevolent,
Harmonious with itfelf and human kind.
Yes—notwithftanding her dark hue, fhe's fair;
If beauty floats not lightly in the fkin,
Nature's mean rind, her garment outermoft,
(To fence the finer teguments defign'd)
Her coat cameleon-like, the changeful fport
Of every colour various light can form,
Imbrown'd by tempefts, blacken'd by rude blows,
By jaundice yellow dy'd, by ficknefs green'd,
By choler crimfon'd, or by terror bleach'd;
Parch'd, rent, and peel'd by Phœbus' burning ray,
Dug by Difeafe, by Labour rough outworn,
Or fhrivell'd by the furly grafp of Age;
Nay, mark'd by Fancy in its embryo ftate:
Shame's writing tablet, Riot's fign-poft coarfe;
Effrontery's armour, Falfehood's bully firm;
And oft of Leprofy the fretwork harfh.

That maid, fuperior to the vulgar throng,
Her tender years in eafe and affluence pafs'd,
The ftaff, the comfort of her parents ag'd,
Their only hope, a numerous progeny
Surviving, while their early fate fhe mourn'd;
Like fome fweet flower, that on its fifter-fhoots,
All blafted in the bud, 'mid varied pomp
Looks fadly down, and fheds a dewy tear.
Why fhould I tell her partnerfhip in woe?
Snatch'd from her father's door by ruffian hands,
Thro' burning defarts rudely was fhe dragg'd
Twelve times an hundred miles, no home to find,
But in this common prifon of her race.
Ill-fated Zilia, what avail'd thofe charms,
That, while they kindled, aw'd the beating hearts
Of Guinea's favage fons, but to provoke
Th' unbridled luft of Britons *civiliz'd*?
Whom kings afpir'd to woo rough feamen fieze,
And fcorning to folicit, boldly rob
Of the laft trace of Freedom's halcyon reign.
By voluntary abftinence perturb'd,
But more by common ravifhment, at length
Her noble foul difdains to exercife
Its functions in a temple fo defil'd.

She, chain'd on deck, her brutal lovers now
Invites to her embrace, her rage to vent
On them incautious; or this boon deny'd,
In fruitlefs vengeance mangles her own limbs.
Then, by extreme exertions overpower'd,
Diffolving into foftnefs, laughs and fings,
Or to the murmuring winds her fate bewails:
Now mourns her parents drown'd in hopelefs grief,
Then her lov'd fwain, to whom her tender vows,
Oft plighted in return, the trufty moon
Alone had witnefs'd. Now fhe fummons him
To refcue her from flavery; then forbids,
Remembering the foul ftain, that marks her out
As pure Love'e antidote. Anon fhe fees
In Fancy's airy fields to venge her rife
Her brothers brave, tho' long by Death difarm'd.

    But who the callous annalift fhall prove
Of every day's deftruction, or narrate
With cold fidelity the havock dire
Of hell-born Av'rice, equally in arms,
Strange policy! againft itfelf and man?
The numberlefs approaches who fhall tell
Of Death relentlefs? whether he attacks
By burning fevers, or by chilling floods,

By wafting illnefs, or a burfting heart,

By gnawing famine, or deep-galling wounds,

By the oppreffor's hands, or by th' opprefs'd.

One night, while darknefs reign'd, the difmal
    clank

Of chains was hear'd, in regular advance.

Two gallant Negroes, not in ftrength impair'd

By pining ficknefs, nor in foul debas'd

By Slavery, their cruel bonds had burft,

And hurried forward their companions chain'd

To the fierce conteft, big with liberty,

Or death lefs dreaded than a fate unknown.

A knife and cutlafs, fecretly procur'd,

With wooden billets, were their only arms.

The trembling guards their weapons prov'd ; but
    foon

By valour overborne, they met their fate;

Or from the giddy tops protection fought.

The decks all clear'd, they to the cabin flew,

On their chief fpoiler to avenge their wrongs,

And with his minions to exchange thofe bonds,

Too long their lot. But while they forward rufh'd

Undaunted, foon their lurking foes, arouz'd

By noife of arms, 'mid the defencelefs throng

Their whizzing meffengers of death difpatch'd
With dreadful fuccefs.   Long th' unequal ftrife
They ftubbornly maintain'd, till by the load
Of irons exhaufted, of their leaders ftript,
By gufhing wounds enervated, by dead
Or dying, link'd to them by common chains,
Entangled, they reluctantly retir'd
To gain a fhort refpite.   Both from above,
And from below, at once their enemies pour'd
On deck, the moment critical to feize,
Immediately its awful weight to lend
To Fate's ftill-wavering balance, and adjudge
To Liberty or Bondage, Life or Death.
Embodied, arm'd, with courage frefh fupply'd,
One volley from their flame-emitting tubes
The rallying fquadron fuddenly difpers'd
To every corner that might cover fhame.
But by their victors re-affembled foon,
A dreadful fcene the glimmering lamps reveal.
From frightful gafhes few exemption boaft.
Some are fo mangled, Avarice itfelf,
With all its over-valuing, fcorns to tempt
The doubtful load.   Without delay it gives
To thefe the brutal mandate to embrace

A watery death. Some inftantly with joy
Obey the fummons. Others only wait
Of friends or kinfmen dear the laft falute :
Then, in their looks difdain and pleafure mix'd,
Hide their disfigur'd limbs 'mid whelming waves.

The prime confpirators, whom battle fpar'd,
Are to a fate more terrible referv'd.
Old tefty Death is bridled, tutor'd, brib'd
To do his office tardily, and try
Experiments of cruelty before
Unpractis'd, to difplay his utmoft fkill .
In chafing Life from every outer work,
Ere he the heart's ftrong garrifon affault.
Now he attacks with torments exquifite
The parts moft fenfible.—But why attempt
The horrid narrative, to human ears,
Itfelf a torment? O'er th' infernal fcene
Her tear-drench'd veil let heav'nly Mercy draw.

Say, barbarous Captain, for thy fell revenge
Their unprovok'd rebellion doft thou plead
As full apology ? But who conferr'd
On thee that right of fovereignty requir'd
To ftamp Rebellion's image on their deeds,
And make them current or in heav'n or earth ?

In what do they man's common rights tranfgrefs ?.

Thou robb'ft them of their Maker's precious boon :

The means moft habile for refuming it

Shall they not ufe ? Doft thou of Freedom boaft,

Thy Britifh birth-right, of the ftruggles great

Made by thy gallant fires to hand it down

To thee entire; yet Africans condemn

For equal ftruggles ? As a fpurious child

Thy country cafts thee out.   Doft plead the price

Thou paid'ft for them ? To whom ? To ravifhers

By thee fuborn'd.   Could they a right confer,

Where they had none themfelves ? Did they not know

A ready market for their villainy,

They of neceffity would ceafe to fpoil.

Wretch, ftay thy cruel hand ; thou art thyfelf

The only rebel, trampling every law

For mankind's blifs by God or man devis'd.

   While regular breezes waft them on their way,

The ftormy iflands rife at length to view,

With joy the longing mariners them hail.

Not fo the flaves.   The hated foil they fpy,

As wretched criminals that awful bar,

Whence every moment they expect their doom.

Forgive them, Britons, tho' they vainly dream,

You tear them from their darling native land,
To make them food for yours. What? is it ftrange,
They thofe as canibals voracious dread,
Whom deftitute of every human fenfe
In all befides experience fad proclaims;
Who with far greater ardor hunt for men
Than they for cattle, Famine's rage to quell?
To pleafe th' unnatural palate tho' you kill'd,
'Twere more compaffion than to fave alive,
Your appetites at fuch.expence to feed.
Forgive this error; 'tis not half fo great
As that concerning them indulg'd by you.
They count you canibals, you count them brutes;
And treat them worfe than all that range your fields.
Or men allow'd, a race they muft be own'd
To you inferior, Nature's vileft dregs,
Her offals foul, the very crudities
Of chaos, that no better form would bear.
Creative Power, forfooth, a fpecies new
Of men muft make for light-complexion'd man
To play the tyrant with, when beafts themfelves
The Heaven-invading rebel's fway renounc'd.

PART III.

THE wifh'd-for haven gain'd, its fhelly bed
The maffive anchors prefs. The trembling flaves
Are hid below, left fharp-ey'd Merchandife
Should thro' their fable covering, threadbare worn,
The whitenefs of their tell-tale bones efpy.
Nor hard were the difcovery; for of fome,
Thro' conftant friction on the naked boards,
Their only bed, and galling of the filth
Worfe than Augean, the prefumptuous bones
Their feeble boundaries fcorn, and gaze abroad;
As weary captives thro' their prifon-grate.
Poor, fcanty remnant of a vigorous fwarm!
The half-chew'd fragments of a thoufand meals
Devouring Death has made, his many mouths
Of melancholy, madnefs, famine, fword,
Scourge, halter, mufket, manifold difeafe
Wide-opening, as his changeful tafte requir'd;
The mangled morfels left to fill his maw,
His appetite when keener! Now they're fed

Moft bounteoufly, yet bounty not the caufe;

Nor for their former miferies remorfe.

When grovelling Avarice herfelf outdoes,

'Tis ftill her own bafe purpofes to ferve.

Like beafts for flaughter, they are fed for fale.

　The ravages of Cruelty repair'd,

Th' inhuman traffic in humanity

Commences; while the miferable ftock

Anew the gauntlet runs, thro' every ftep

Of galling ignominy trac'd before

Ev'n at the goal of Slavery's career

Unlimited, unpitied, unrepaid.

Hark! how the bawling Auctioneer proclaims

The varying price of blood, the purchafers

Meanwhile contending, who fhall moft debafe

In value that high nature moft of all

Debas'd in them, and at the meaneft rate

Their great Creator's fullied image buy.

All-gracious Heav'n! can this that nature be

For which thou Earth didft wed and give thy life,

Price infinite! for ranfom, which is here

Sold fo contemptuoufly for Earth's mere drofs?

Are thefe, in this ftrange trade engag'd, the men

Who tell the world their faith, that Thou for man,

Without regard to nation, tongue, or clime,
Didſt purchaſe freedom endleſs and ſupreme?
In their profeſſion, ſurely, they but ſport
With credulous minds. How elſe would they
          preſume
Thoſe to enſlave to whom thou ſay'ſt, " Be free?"
    Or of the brutal *ſcramble* is the ſcene
Unfeelingly prepar'd? The fearful ſlaves
In an apartment cloſ'd, where darkneſs reigns,
The unknown iſſue wait. A ſignal giv'n,
The ardent purchaſers, with ropes ſupply'd,
Ruſh in, and circle in their ample graſp
Without diſtinction all they can ſurpriſe.
But of the miſerable captives who
Can tell th' unequall'd terror, when theſe hounds
Bloodthirſty, firm, impetuous, are looſ'd
On them, ſecluded from all means of flight
Or ſelf-defence? A univerſal ſhriek
Immediately th' aſtoniſh'd welkin rends.
The timid women for protection fly
To thoſe by nature their protectors fram'd.
Some, ſwooning, for a while their ſpirits loſe;
While others loſe them, ne'er to be recall'd.
The men themſelves, who hitherto contemn'd

The moſt outrageous thruſts of tyranny,
This ſhock, th' apparent criſis of their fate,
Unable to ſuſtain, in every limb
Now trembling to each other cling, that aid
Imploring others vainly crave from them.
A juſt reſemblance of the dreadful ſcene
Where can I find? All Nature it diſclaims.
The moſt ferocious animals would ſcorn
Such wanton cruelty. Ingenious Art
Hath in this ſtrange device herſelf outdone.

But when Diſeaſe refuſes to deſert
His ſtrong intrenchments 'midſt the captive crew,
Not terrified by phyſic's power combin'd,
Nor by the gentler hand of Nature lur'd,
Medicinal viands bearing; many hang
A hopeleſs burden on their tyrant's board.
The fix'd expence of ſale their niggard price
Would fail to reimburſe, and miniſh much
That ſhare of gain the lower orders claim,
As faithful ſatellites of tyranny;
Each in his various orb revolving round
His lordly center, in reſemblance ſtrict,
With ſyſtematic nhumanity.
Ah! doubly wretched! what then is your fate,

By Avarice infatiate at all points
Outrageoufly affail'd! A bleft abode
It in your country would no longer deign;
And now into its own peculiar foil
Denies admiffion. Sure, they are not fold;
Nor do they e'er revifit Afric's fhore.

The love of human nature o'er their fate
Would draw the veil of darknefs; but ftern Truth
Burfts boldy thro', and to the view amaz'd
Reveals thefe wretches ftarving in the fhips,
Or 'midft the weak efforts of dubious life
Struggling for permanence, tofs'd overboard;
The recompence of faithful fellow-fharks,
Their allies following from their native fhores.

'Mongft various colonies difpers'd, new fcenes
Of mifery them await. The cruel foil,
As of her lords the fpirit fhe imbib'd,
The yearly facrifice of thoufands claims.
Nor may a tithe her appetite fuffice.
The third or fourth of Guinea's fons alone
She deigns as regular firft-fruits to receive,
Oblation for the reft, who ftill muft yield
Her homage, and refpite from Death procure
By grappling with indigenous Difeafe,

And proof of ſtrength ſuperior to its rage.

   One day, while noontide's ſcorching violence
    chac'd
The fainting labourers to a cooling ſhade,
Whoſe kind vicinity invited them
Under its pitying covert to devour
Their lean repaſt, approach'd the mournful band
A ſervant of that Sovereign who proclaims
To captives liberty. With ſoul ſincere
Long had he wiſhed his tidings full of grace
To theſe poor captive Heathens to declare,
And ſave from ſlavery at leaſt their ſouls,
Long had he labour'd with their rugged lord
Th' alleviation of their bonds to gain,
But ſtill his gentle ſoul beneath its load
Of ſorrow groan'd. To them Philander thus:

   " Hail! brethren of the common ſtock of man!
Your bonds I wail, and in your ſorrows join;
But though from country, kindred, friends belov'd,
Sever'd by ſeas immenſe, a gleam of light
Breaks through your darkneſs. Had your native land
Retain'd you ſtill, your bodies had been free;
But never had you heard of liberty
Far more exalted, for the ſoul procur'd

By Him who claims not Afric's plains alone,
But all the world as his dominion wide.
Forfake your Idols, and that Faith embrace
Alone divine, the mildeft known to man.

A univerfal figh, as by confent,
Th' ungracious tidings anfwer'd. Downcaft looks
And gloomy filence their rejection feal'd.
At length, a female, in whofe piercing eye,
To former miferies retrofpective, flam'd
Awaking indignation, filence broke.

" Calypfo once in pleafures unalloy'd
Liv'd unfufpicious, of her friends the joy,
The right hand of her hufband, pride of fons.
But while fhe courted on the river's brink
The fanning breeze, and hugg'd her fmiling babe,
A crew in arms appear'd. In vain fhe try'd
To 'fcape them, or the adjacent village roufe.
Fond hufband! tender fons! I blame you not.
Calypfo's ftifled cries ye could not hear.
My frighten'd fuckling join'd alone in grief,
By its heart-piercing fcreams; while, fwooning, I
Was bound and tofs'd aboard the hoftile barge.
One night, as on the leaky boards I lay,
And vainly ftrove to foothe my crying babe,

Half-chok'd with water dafh'd from fide to fide,
My wrathful fpoiler, in his fleep difturb'd,
Tore from my arms my helplefs innocent;
And——oh! my limbs ftill quiver, while I tell
The horrid deed — he plung'd it 'midft the ftream.
'Gainft Heav'n no African had thus rebell'd.
He was a Chriftian, boafted of his name,
And in reply to all my bitter plaints,
My infant curs'd for Heathen unbaptiz'd.
Such was his mercy, fuch the baptifm
He gave my babe, and fuch the powerful means
He us'd to win me to his *better* faith.

   " Few days I in the floating prifon pafs'd,
To which they wafted me, till of my fate
My hufband, and the firft-born of his race,
The partners fad my doubtful eyes beheld.
What warring paffions rack'd my beating breaft!
Joy and amazement, love and terror mix'd!
The felfifh joy, that promis'd fome folace
From partnerfhip in fufferings, check'd anon
More generous forrow for the hopelefs fate
Of thofe fo dear, and anguifh for the reft,
By fpoilers murder'd, or by famine gnaw'd.
Poor, pity-pleading orphans, on a world

H

Unpitying left, or by their country fav'd,
Yet only fav'd that Chriftians may deftroy!

" My mournful night a ray of joy illum'd
Still in my fea-borne dungeon, while I knew,
A treafure it contain'd to me fo dear.
At laft, when for the dreaded fale prepar'd,
Calypfo hop'd her lot would common be
With thofe fhe lov'd. But ah! the dire command,
To part for ever, harfhly was announc'd.
In unknown language mercy we implor'd,
We clafp'd our tyrants' knees, and kifs'd their feet,
And to each other clung in fond embrace,
With all the violence of defpairing love.
But us the unrelenting lafh disjoin'd
Never to meet again, till friendly Death
Us to our country, free from care, reftore.
Already there rejoices my lov'd lord
With his forefathers on their blifsful plains.
For madden'd by defpair and rage, next day
He threw away that life he fcorn'd to fpend
In ferving him our facred bonds who burft.
My fon's fate Fame hath never yet propall'd.

" But why on perfonal fufferings enlarge?
Thefe are but fcraps of mifery, crumbs of woe,

'That fall from Cruelty's expenfive board ;
The gleanings of her harveft, with the heaps
Her greedy fcythe cuts down at once compar'd.
Twelve times eleven captives, in three funs,
Alive intomb'd 'midft gorging waves I faw.
Their murderers charg'd them with no other crime
Than ficknefs, their own cruelty the caufe.
Then call not, Chriftian, thy religion mild,
Since fuch its fruits.   If mild, 'twould doubtlefs
    tame
Thofe favage monfters that our race purfue.
Say not, thy God gives freedom to the foul ;
While all his worfhippers, within our ken,
Are flaves to every vice.   This liberty,
By thee extoll'd, will he on none beftow
But thofe whofe bodies are in bondage held ?
Is this the price he for his boon demands ?
Does he empower his fervants firft to rob
Of every prefent bleffing, and torment
With every curfe this life can wreftle with,
Thofe to them guiltlefs; then their griefs to mock
With meagre hopes of bleffings in that ftate,
Oppreffion's rod that from the tyrant wrefts ?
Thy faith's a lie, or thou defam'ft thy God."

Philander, ſtruggling to ſuppreſs the tears
Compaſſion crav'd for human miſeries,
And heart-felt ſorrow for th' expoſure ſoul
Of Chriſtianity to Heatheniſh ſcorn,
With labouring breaſt reply'd ; " Such floods of woe,
Let looſe by faithleſs Chriſtians, have on thee
Their fury pour'd, and ſuch the dreadful ſcenes
Thou haſt been witneſs to, I ſcarce admire
Thy groſs miſapprehenſions of our faith.
To Slavery no auſpicious look it lends.
Ev'n at its root a deadly blow it aims :
Commanding every ſoul, without reſerve,
To love his neighbour as himſelf he loves ;
And whatſoever he from others claims,
To them in every act of life to yield :
Love univerſal, conſtant and ſincere,
Demanding as its proof, adorning, end,
The ſole completion of its heav'n-taught law,
Some who this faith profeſs are cruel, falſe,
Unjuſt and impious, but itſelf diſclaims
All ſuch profeſſors as its greateſt foes,
Who under friendſhip's veil its vitals pierce.
Judge not of all who bear the Chriſtian name
By your oppreſſors : happy Britain owns

Far other men, who live as they believe,
Who Slavery curfe, and for your Freedom ftrive."
  " Delude us not," fhe cry'd, " the fame dark hue
Of foul all Chriftians marks, the common mafs
One gall embitters; ev'n the hated name
Bears poifon in it.   Were it borne by me
Calypfo would herfelf be cruel, falfe,
Unjuft and impious, would her God blafpheme,
Abjure her chaftity and trade in blood.
Were Britons better than our tyrants here,
The very name of Slavery they would
Exterminate.   If fome of them are friends
To helplefs Africans, few muft they be,
Elfe us from fetters would their friendfhip loofe.
If ftarving Negroe fteals a bit of bread,
And parts it with his fpoufe, fhe's flogg'd with him,
Altho' fhe only ate of what he ftole.
But Britons call our murderers their fons;
They fend them food; their fcourges they provide;
They eat the produce of our wafted ftrength;
Nay, to this fea-girt prifon us convey.
Our groans affail them 'mid their feafts of joy,
And fwell the gales that fan their diftant land;
Our tears increafe the tides that lafh their fhores;

Our blood pollutes the luxuries they devour.
Yes, Britons are our tyrants, while they fmile
On thofe who tyrannize! 'Tis Britain's gold
That bribes our kinfmen us to fteal and fell;
'Tis Britain's fcourge that flays us; 'tis her rod,
O'er countlefs billows reaching, to the ground
That fmites us down; there her foot tramples us;
Her hand lif 's pittance fnatches from our lips;
Her fword relentlefs fheds our guiltlefs blood."

    All his efforts to win Calypfo vain,
Philander to another captive turn'd,
Whofe mein fuperior feem'd, whofe penfive eye
Spoke keen attention.   " Many are," he faid,
" Your prefent woes, but thofe who Afric know
As more fevere your former lot defcribe.
Your Mafters give you gardens of your own.
A day of reft in feven our holy law
To you vouchfafes.   Your liberty you may
At length acquire.   Your joy you oft proclaim
In focial mufic, or the fprightly dance,"

    'Twas Ephraim he addrefs'd, of Calabar,
Whofe fate his labours to that glebe confin'd.
With fcornful fmile he faid, " They doubtlefs fport
With your credulity fuch tales who vend.

If such our blifs in this unnatural foil,
Why with such ardor pant we for our own?
Why on the ocean fo intenfely gaze?
Why kifs the fands to Africa moft nigh,
And hug the waves that may have wafh'd her fhore?
Our babes why welcome we with tears alone,
And grace the funerals of our friends with joy
In all its tranfports? Death why covet more
Than all the treafures of our griping lords?
Why meet it with a fmile, and when our hopes
It trifles with, accelerate its pace?
Are thefe the tokens of fuperior blifs?
Harfh labour never ruffled Ephraim's hand;
But now its flender bones are oft laid bare.
Beneath the burden vile his back ne'er bow'd :
Now 'tis fo bow'd he cannot ftand upright.
His fhadow in its weary path his eye
Sees flowly moving, like a willow bent
Before the bluftering blaft, and threatening ftill
To hide its weaknefs in the weeping brook.
  " Four times four hours of labour every day
Our cruel lord requires, and fcarcely deigns
A fhort refpite our fcanty meals to gorge.
When night relieves us from our daily tafk,

Some hours our own neceffities demand.
Exhaufted, we thro' dreary wilds muft crawl,
While not a gleam the circling veil pervades,
And gather twigs our viands mean to drefs,
And warm our limbs with toil and wet benumb'd.
Five fleeting hours for flumber fcarce remain;
And from this niggard boon the ceafelefs mills
Oft borrow a large portion, ne'er repaid.
If fleep be banifh'd, feeble is our ftrength
For next day's labour. If its balmy pow'rs
We welcome, oft a precious limb the price.
Our garments fcarcely fkreen us from the blaft.
Our food the tie reluctantly maintains
'Twixt foul and body. With their liberal gift
Of gardens ftill our tyrants us upbraid.
But what are thefe? Our country's wilds fupply'd
Our calls more amply, of their own accord.
Thefe narrow fpots fome vegetables yield,
Which yet unripe we greedily devour
To ftill the rage of hunger, tho' affur'd
That thus when ftill'd, in manifold difeafe
A fatal vent more furioufly it feeks.

  " If fleep fome moments from our mafter fteals,

If weaknefs fpreads its languor o'er our toil,
Or fcanty feem our grafs-loads, twice a day,
With fpeechlefs labour for the cattle glean'd
In various tracts of defart, blade by blade;
For haplefs Negro no excufe is heard.
Our limbs the ruthlefs lafh excoriates,
And to the bones refiftlefs digs its way.
At work oft fainting, I have found with joy
My fpirit on the wing, its parting thought
Immediately my diftant fires to join.
Illufion fond and fleeting! Soon again
I into life have cruelly been lafh'd.
Its hideous fmack, inceffant thro' the day,
Is our chief mufic. Now and then the fong,
Or dance we meafure; gaiety not the caufe,
But fond folicitude to banifh grief,
Tho' for a moment only. That we may
Our liberty at length procure, you boaft.
We may indeed; but only when our toil
The tax defrays not; when its value's fled
With youth, and ftrength, and joy; when hafty
    Death
Threatens to rob our tyrants of their cofts,
And as a boon that liberty beftows

They afk a price for.   Weekly days of reft
Enjoy we alfo; but in name alone.
Ye Chriftians fay, ye confecrate thefe days
In honour of your God, while ye enforce
Our profanation; for on them muft we
Our daily toil in gathering grafs purfue,
And then our gardens cultivate, or ftarve.
Curs'd African! no fcorn nor cruelty
For thee fuffices! Oft thy ears are flit
For mere diftinction.   Ev'n thy life fo vile,
That Chriftian juftice for its ravifhment
To claim a reparation fcarcely deigns.
But hark! our tafkmafter's harfh cry refounds!
The moments ftol'n our ftripes muft reimburfe.
Chriftian, farewell! thy faith I ftill difclaim,
'Till its blind votaries learn the love of man."
   But ah! the fhriek of African diftrefs
Is not to Caribbean Ifles confin'd.
I hear it echoed thro' Columbia's plains
And wilds immeafurable.   Can it be?
Sure, 'tis fome ftrange illufion on the ear!
Can thofe, who in the caufe of Liberty
Life's nobleft channels emptied, claim a right
To drain the ciftern of a Negro's heart.

In Slavery's conftant wafte? Yet fuch their claim.
Myriads of Negroes muft be facrific'd
In ferving a new fenfe, a tafte acquir'd
By violence done to Nature. Could that box,
The pungent herb containing, be fupply'd
No otherwife, in wrath and horror I
Would caft it from me, as a new Pandora's,
Fell fource of ills, not only to a world
Grown old in wickednefs, but to the new.
Hath Hell created this additional tafte,
Man to deftroy by moft unlikely means,
And to its bitter fcorn both worlds expofe?

   Columbia's gallant fons! is Liberty
That prize ineftimable fought by you
At fuch expence? Then to your fellow-men
Impart it generoufly, elfe every man
Muft difbelieve that Freedom was your end.
To turbulence, injuftice, luft of pow'r
Your deeds fhall be afcrib'd. For who can dream
That thofe by love of Liberty fincere
Are animated, brethren who enflave?
Your fufferings under Britain's broken yoke
Delineate to the utmoft bounds of Truth,
All adding that as probable was fear'd;

Still with your own dark vaſſalage compar'd,
Ye had been free.   Do ye to Heav'n remit
Oblations grateful for its precious gift?
All theſe as inſincere it ſpurns, and you
Accuſes of ingratitude extreme,
Its common boon while ye monopolize.

　　Your treaſury of its ſcanty ſums why drain
In this expenſive trade? Why ſtock your lands
With muſhroom-men, mere tenants of a day,
Whoſe blanks inceſſantly muſt be ſupply'd
By recent purchaſe, in their offspring who
Themſelves perpetuate not? A nation's wealth
In its extent of population lies;
And freeborn men alone will populate.
Tho' others ſhould, to cultivate your lands
Muſt Africa be made a wilderneſs?
Say, can it not ſuffice, that of your ſoil
The better half already hath been drench'd
With that offenceleſs blood itſelf had nurs'd?
Muſt diſtant continents their victims lend
To ſaturate the other, and awake
The heav'n-arouſing cry of blood from both?
How can ye to your ſons a love ſincere
Of Liberty tranſmit while they 'mong ſlaves

Are born, and from their very cradles taught
To trample on their fellow-men as worms?
Each flave you purchafe, at the very heart
Of Liberty a mortal thruft ye aim.
Nay, do ye not a heritage of guilt
To fons tranfmit, and fondly ferve them heirs
To that dread vengeance, which may them at length
Subject to Slavery. Juftly might ye fear,
A race of tyrants for your future fons
Ye now prepar'd; did not your cruelty,
Here only politic, their growth prevent.

　Why fled your fathers to a diftant foil?
The yoke of Slavery was it not to 'fcape?
And can ye hope your freedom to maintain
By making others flaves? Opprefs ye not
The ftranger, for ye know a ftranger's heart,
Wifhful, perplex'd, and aching; wavering ftill
'Twixt feeble hope and fear predominant;
For in that land by you as lords poffefs'd,
Like wretched Negroes, ftrangers once were ye.

　Friends! Britons! Chriftians! Men' by what
　　dear name
Shall I the audience of your hearts invoke,
And your extreme exertions fupplicate

For helplefs Africans ?   Can Intereft weigh ?
Then ftop th' expenditure of countlefs fums
In this vile trade ; the national lofs prevent
Of thoufands of your gallant mariners,
Your natural guardians, by difeafe or want,
Inhuman ftripes or African revenge.
A trade why idolize, of every vice
Prolific nurfery ; that a race remits
Of tyrants, rich indeed, but with the fpoils
Of innocents; a race of brutal lords,
Of cruel hufbands, and unfeeling fires ;
A race of murderers, foon to undermine
The very bafe of all religion, law,
And freedom, public or domeftic weal ?
Heav'n's execration muft that commerce mark,
The feed of enmity that fcatters wide
Through peaceful nations, and all bonds diffolves
'Twixt friends and brethren. Muft a continent vaft,
For the mere luxuries of a petty ifle,
Be piecemeal facrific'd ?   Exclaim no more
'Gainft Spain's dread cruelties, that a new world
Depopulated, while yourfelves, alike
In Mammon's worfhip madden'd, wafte the old.
Her fword is fheath'd, but Britain's ftill devours.

Sure, Hell incens'd at the defection vaft
Of human victims Chriftian fhrines that ftain'd,
Through the new dawn of Evangelic light,
This traffick hath devis'd, in Heathenifh blood
Its loffes to repair, and on thofe pow'rs
Who its fell domination have abjur'd
Itfelf avenges, them its murdering tools
In this new haveck making.   Boldly join
Againft this commerce infamous, that makes
The name of *Chriftian*, nobleft borne by man,
A ftench to Heathen blind, and bids him fay
In cruel fcorn, with any crime when charg'd ;
" What ?   Do you take me for a Chriftian vile ?"
A commerce—bearing in its very form
An abjuration of the Chriftian name ;
Nay, of humanity !   The great efforts
Of Courts your facred interefts who guard,
Of learned Seminaries mark with awe ;
And let the venerable Senate hear
Your voice unanimous.   Then other Sharpes,
Ramfays, and Clarkfons fhall their ftrength combine
To ftop the fweeping torrent.   For your fins
Vain your pretences to afflict your fouls,
And jointly deprecate th' Almighty's wrath.

Ah ! is not this the faſt by him requir'd ?
Free'y the bonds of wickedneſs to looſe,
The load inſufferable to remove,
To bid the oppreſs'd go free, and every yoke
To break in pieces ? Is it not to feed
The ſtarving wretch, the outcaſt to receive
Within thy ſhelter, nakedneſs to clothe,
And from *thy own fleſh* not thyſelf to hide ?

But chiefly ye, great Senators, whoſe nod
Imperial gives to nations bleſſed peace,
Or war's dread ruin ; ſlavery to the free,
Or freedom to the fetter'd ſlave; give ear !
The cry of miſery from your hallowed walls
Exclude not.   Wretched fellow-men implore.
Tho' gods by office, ye like them muſt die.
Tho' abject worms are they, of pain or bliſs
Yet equally ſuſceptible with you.
Them ſcorn not as by native ſlavery
Degraded.   Stepdame-like hath Nature ſtamp'd
Of infamy ſome marks infallible
On their nativity ?   With yokes of iron
Around their necks, or fetters on their limbs,
Light inauſpicious did they firſt behold ?
Foes to mankind are their own kings ? What then ?

Muſt ye from them your juriſprudence learn?
But is not Slavery lawleſs? To deprive
The innocent of Freedom, treaſon fell
'Gainſt Nature's law, the univerſal bond?
Such reaſoning ought a Briton to rejeƈt
With indignation. Who hath made you free?
Sure, that great Parent, who to every child
This as his rightful patrimony gives.
If others loſe it by oppreſſion foul,
Muſt ye confirm the robbery? Ought ye not,   '
As thoſe by Freedom's tie alone who hold
Your high preferments, rather from the hand
Of Tyrants the oppreſſive rod to pluck?
But many once were free, now bound by you,
Judg'd by their own laws, by their *Purrow* rul'd,
Their parliament, whoſe members they had choſe.
Tho' under Tyrants ſome were born, their loins
Were lighter than your finger: their great aim
In making ſlaves, your yawning yokes to fill.
" But they were criminals." What law of your's
Had they tranſgreſs'd? If ſome were juſtly doom'd
By their own lords, yet criminals to you
They could not be. Thoſe only could inflict
The puniſhment, who had the wrong receiv'd.

K

'The work of Mercy truft not in the hands
Of rugged Planters, nor the hope indulge
That they from principles of intereft true,
From fhame, remorfe, or pity will reform.
So blind, beyond the prefent moment's gain
They cannot look ; for guilt no blufhes know;
Their callous hearts compunctions never twinge;
Nor yearn their bowels, but on gilded duft.
The gloomy Ethiop, groaning as their flave,
As foon his fkin fhall change, as they, fo long
The flaves of wickednefs, fhall juftice learn !
   The dictates of falfe policy difclaim.
Tho' bars eternal on this trade were laid,
And liberty to every wretch proclaim'd ;
Were population cherifh'd, wages giv'n,
And lands allotted as their property
Unalienable ; thofe fo kindly woo'd
Would call your colonies their better home,
Your planters parents, and their work perform
With chearfulnefs.   A nation new would rife
Their narrow limits fcarcely could contain.
No more of infurrections would ye hear,
Of runaways, of proffer'd price for blood.
Your intereft would be theirs.   But for a time

Tho' trade fhould fuffer, is not rectitude
That policy alone from hazard free?
Your treafury with th' unlawful price of blood
Would ye replenifh? Can the righteous Lord
Delight in aught but juftice? This alone
Exalts a nation; fin a foul reproach
To any people, to whatever height
Of glory rais'd. Far greater now your guilt
This trade in tolerating, than before,
Its wickednefs unthought of, unexplor'd,
And its extent unknown. The piteous cry
Of wretched Africans is Nature's voice
To you as parents; nay, the voice of God
To you as children of one common fire.

Oh! for one moment of compaffion, deem
Thefe as your fons, from your embraces torn,
Dragg'd to a diftant land, in fetters bound,
With toil and hunger wafted, beaten, lafh'd,
And often murder'd with impunity!
What poignancy of anguifh would ye feel!
What would ye not for their deliverance dare?
Your fons they are, while of this empire wide
Ye are the common parents, bound to reach
To every fuffering child your equal arm.

The time may be, when ev'n your natural fons,
Your hope, joy, pride, perpetual, dearer felves
May under mercilefs oppreffors groan.
Ah ! could ye fee it, what then would ye wifh
To Negroes ye had done ; for ever loft
The glorious opportunity ? At once
The cry of African and Indian blood
Your walls re-echo ; nay, it Heav'n hath reach'd,
And if your ears ye ftop, fhall vengeance dread
And fudden on your guilty heads bring down
From its impartial bar.　This cry reject,
And thus to Slavery fons unborn confign.

　　The threatenings of the Univerfal Judge
Ye judges of the earth with trembling hear !
" If ye JEHOVAH's voice of precept fcorn,
" Your fons and daughters fhall be captive led.*
" Ye kine of Bafhan, who the poor opprefs
" And crufh the needy ; by his holinefs
" The God of Heav'n hath fworn : the days ap-
　　　proach
" When you, and your pofterity, like fifh,
" He fhall with hooks from your poffeffions drag. †
" Who others captive leads, himfelf fhall go
" Into captivity."‡　Heav'n's equal law is this.

　　* Deut. xxviii. 15, 32, 46.　† Am. iv. 12.　‡ Rev. xiii. 10.

'On every nation known to Hiftory's page,
Whofe hands were with Oppreffion's fruits defil'd,
The vials of his indignation dread
Hath he not emptied ; ev'n on Jacob's fons,
His favourite race ? Have ye alone receiv'd
Indemnity, or fome all-powerful fpell
Difcover'd 'gainft the thunder-bolts of Heav'n ?
Ah ! no. Thofe fields with Heathen blood bedew'd
Already hath the blood of Chriftians drench'd.
JEHOVAH's wrath Columbia's plains yet tell,
Where with the mother and her daughter he
His quarrel pleaded ; arming fons 'gainft fires,
And brother againft brother. As the caufe
Your impious commerce fain would ye difown.
But 'tis from Heav'n's great regifter proclaim'd ;
" Becaufe they wickednefs have plow'd, and reap'd
" Iniquity, the mother hath been dafh'd
" In pieces on her children.* As the fire,
" Your wickednefs around you hath devour'd ;
" For fuel therefore fhall the people be :
" No man in pity fhall his brother fpare."†
    Oft are not your plantations vifited

---

* Hof. xiii. 14.   † Ifa. ix. 18, 19. x. 14.

With dreadful hurricanes ; the fields laid wafte,

The houfes fwept away, th' inhabitants

'Mid ruins buried, and your trading fhips

Dafh'd one againft another, or devour'd

By yawning billows ? Britons, then give ear

To th' awful voice of an incenfed God.

It bellows in the thunder, in the ftorm

It rages, in the fweeping torrent roars.

The forked lightnings are his arrows feil ;

The dreadful balls of fire, that round you burft

'Midft horrid darknefs, are his meffengers

Of indignation.   Thus thofe fruits he blafts,

Rear'd on Oppreffion's ftem ; thofe ftately domes,

Built with the fpoils of innocents, deftroys ;

Confumes thofe fields by guiltlefs blood enrich'd ;

Thofe veffels, gaping to devour the gain-

Of robbery, wrecks ; the fpoilers oft themfelves

Involv'd in ruin with their curfed fpoils.

His juftice can ye charge, or difavow

Such vifitations as its awful proofs ?

To " rain a tempeft horrible on thofe

" Who violence love ;" hath not th' Eternal vow'd,

" Becaufe he loveth right ?"† The heritage

† Pf. xi. 6, 7.

" Of the oppreſſor from th' Almighty this ;

" Unſtable, like the moth's, his houſe he builds.

" Like ruſhing waters, terrors on him ſeize.

" Him in the night a tempeſt ſteals away :

" The boiſterous Eaſt-wind forces him along,

" And from his place him into darkneſs hurls."‡

Thus did he viſit Egypt's land of ſlaves, -

When claiming liberty for his oppreſs'd.

" With hail their vines, with froſt their ſycamores

" He blaſted ; to the ſtorm their cattle gave,

" And to the burning thunder-bolts their flocks :

" On them the fierceneſs of his wrath he caſt."‖

    " This, ye who ſwallow up the needy, hear :

" Who ſell the poor for ſilver, or exchange

" In traffick vile ; the great JEHOVAH ſwears :

" I, ſurely, none of all your impious deeds

" Will e'er forget. Shall not the land for this

" Be ſeiz'd with trembling ? Every tenant mourn ?

" My anger in the ſwelling flood ſhall riſe ;

" And as by Egypt's troubled ſtream, the ſoil

" Shall from its place be torn, and 'midſt the waves

‡ Job xxvii. 13, 18, 20, 21. ‖ Pſ. lxxviii. 47, 49.

" Be buried.   Ev'n at noon the fun afham'd
" Shall veil his head, and in the cloudlefs day
" The earth in horrid darknefs will I hide."*

* Am. viii. 4, 6, 9.

FINIS.

www.ingramcontent.com/pod-product-compliance
Lightning Source LLC
Chambersburg PA
CBHW030008030726
47499CB00008B/2953